BIG WORDS
small stories

THE
TRAVELING
DUSTBALL

For Isaac, Leni, Eleanor and Reis — J.H.

For my aunts and uncles — T.L.M.

Text © 2019 Judith Henderson
Illustrations © 2019 Trenton McBeath

Kids Can Press gratefully acknowledges the financial support of the Government of Ontario, through the Ontario Media Development Corporation; the Ontario Arts Council; the Canada Council for the Arts; and the Government of Canada for our publishing activity.

Published in Canada and the U.S. by Kids Can Press Ltd.
25 Dockside Drive, Toronto, ON M5A 0B5

Kids Can Press is a Corus Entertainment Inc. company

www.kidscanpress.com

The artwork in this book was rendered in graphite pencil and colored in Photoshop.
The text is set in Bizzle-Chizzle.

Edited by Yasemin Uçar
Designed by Julia Naimska

Printed and bound in Malaysia, in 10/2018 by Tien Wah Press (Pte.) Ltd.

CM 19 0 9 8 7 6 5 4 3 2 1

Library and Archives Canada Cataloguing in Publication

Henderson, Judith, author
     The traveling dustball / written by Judith Henderson ; illustrated by T. L. McBeth.

(Big words small stories ; 2)
Short stories.
ISBN 978-1-77138-789-7 (hardcover)

     1. Readers (Elementary). I. McBeth, T. L., illustrator II. Title.

PE1117.H462 2019   428.6'2   C2018-902015-6

G WORDS

mall stories

THE
TRAVELING DUSTBALL

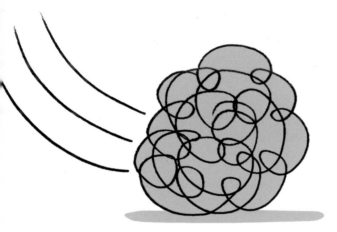

WHAAAAA!

Written by **Judith Henderson**

Illustrated by **T. L. McBeth**

KIDS CAN PRESS

Table of Contents

Who's Who

This is Davey. He likes to travel.

Abigail, not so much.

This is the Sprinkle Fairy.

She has a word factory in Sicily. That's where the best words in the world come from.

ITALY

Sicily

These are the Sprinklers. They're the Sprinkle Fairy's helpers.

They sprinkle Big Words into small places. If you happen to spot a Sprinkler in a story, it means there's a Big Word coming!

BIG WORD!

"Use the Big Words, then see what happens."

The Traveling Dustball

"Abigail, have you ever wondered about dust bunnies?"

"No."

"I mean, where do they come from? Why do they hide under the bed?"

"Can we talk about this later? I'm trying to read."

"Okay. Don't mind me."

"MUST you?"

"Big Word coming. BIG!"

"Someone has to sweep up the dust bunnies."

"Well, it's *irksome*."

"**IRKSOME!**
Big Word! Big Word!"

"Yes, irksome."

Say it: URK-sum

IRKSOME is a Big Word that means annoying.

Spaghetti and Meatballs

"You can travel anywhere with a dustball. You can go to the store or even float to Italy."

YAWN!

"Is Italy far? Because I was about to take a nap."

"It's just across the ocean."

Pump!

Pump!

"Oh boy. Here we go again."

"Hi, Sprinkle Fairy. We're going to Italy."

"Me, too! Maybe I'll see you there."

"Italy looks
very busy."

"Whoops."

"Move your
dust-a-ball!"

"Mamma
mia!"

HONK!

HONK!

20

"BROUHAHA!

Big Word! Big Word!"

"Looks like you two are in a bit of a pickle."

"Sprinkle Fairy, can you help us?"

"Yes. I'll be right back."

21

"I'll have twenty-six orders of spaghetti and meatballs to go, please."

"LUNCH IS READY!"

"Ahhh ..."

"Mmmm ..."

"Yummy."

"You'd better get going while the going is good."

"Okay, but can I get a doggie bag for these meatballs?"

"Bye, everybody! Drive safely!"

BROUHAHA is a Big Word
that means a noisy, excited
reaction to something.

The Big Wave

"Abigail! Stop **lollygagging!**"

"It's nap time."

"LOLLYGAGGING!
Big Word! Big Word!"

"Go get your swimsuit while I get the dustball ready!"

Pump!

Pump!

Say it: LAW-lee-gag-ing

29

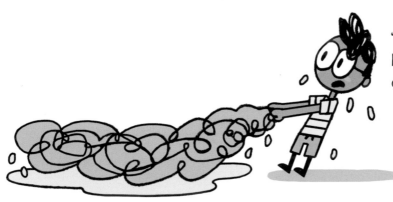

LOLLYGAGGING is a Big Word
that means spending time doing not
much of anything.

Cloud Tea

"Davey? I can't go anywhere today. I don't feel well."

"What's wrong?"

RUMBLE! BUMPLE! GRUMPLE!

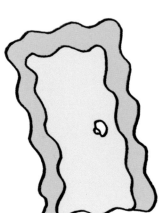

"What was that?!"

"Big Word coming. BIG!"

"My tummy has the collywobbles."

"COLLYWOBBLES! Big Word! Big Word!"

34

"Davey, I need Cloud Tea for my collywobbles. We're all out."

"Okay. I'll go to China."

Pump!

Pump!

"Hi, Sprinkle Fairy. I'm going to China for Cloud Tea. Abigail has the collywobbles."

"You're almost there. Just ask for Mr. Shi Wu ... See you!"

"Hello. Are you Mr. Shi Wu?"

"Are you looking for Cloud Tea?"

"Yes, please. My friend has the collywobbles."

"Ah, yes. Cloud Tea is good for collywobbles. I have a fresh batch all ready."

"Tell your friend to take two and call me in the morning."

"Thanks."

36

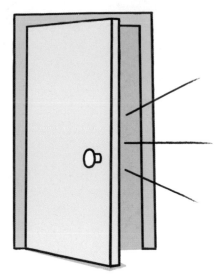

"Is that you, Davey? Did you get the tea?!"

"Coming!"

"You're looking better already. No more collywobbles?"

Slurp!

"Nope. I feel great!"

"Abigail, you're floating!"

"Maybe you put in too much cloud."

37

COLLYWOBBLES is a Big Word
that means a sore or upset tummy.

The Stinky Cheese

40

"Is that a problem?"

"It's horrible! Our fresh mountain air smells like stinky feet!"

"Something definitely stinks here."

"Nobody can smell my wonderful chocolate because Mr. Pinky's cheese is so stinky!"

"But you haven't even tasted my cheese!"

"I don't need to. It smells bad!"

BAAAD

"I'll taste it."

"Really?"

"Better him
than me."

BAAAD

"It's ... it's *delicious*! Here, Abigail. Try some."

"No, thanks. Uh-uh. Nope."

"Mr. Fudge?"

"Well, all right ..."

BAAAD

"I'll try some."

"Oh my. It *is* good! How could something so stinky taste so good?"

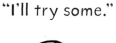

"Okay, fine. Me, too."

"Big Word coming! BIG!"

"Mmmm ..."

"Very, very good."

"Yum."

"Huh."

"It smells really bad, but it tastes really good. What an interesting *phenomenon*."

"PHENOMENON! Big Word! Big Word!"

44

PHENOMENON is a Big Word
that means something that happens
that is unusual or interesting and
makes people curious.

IRKSOME

BROUHAHA

PHENOMENON

LOLLYGAGGING

COLLYWOBBLES

"It's time for our Play on Words! Everybody ready?"

"READY!"

"Lights! Camera! Action!"

48

GASP!

"Oh my!"

"My goodness!"

"What is this BROUHAHA?"

"It is very IRKSOME to be woken up in the middle of the night."

"It's giving me the COLLYWOBBLES."

"It's a PHENOMENON! Everybody, come quickly!"

"Let's all go see the phenomenon! No LOLLYGAGGING!"

49

"Ooooh ..."

"Abigail is sleepwalking."

"How does she do it?"

"I don't know."

"It's an interesting PHENOMENON."

The End.

Also available in the
Big Words Small Stories series:

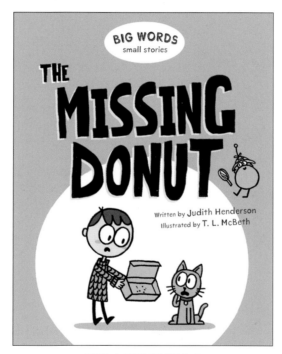

978-1-77138-788-0

"A HUMDINGER for budding wordplay fans."
— *Booklist*

D0520714